1. Folklore
2. Animals - Folklore

W9-CTU-313

8

DATE DUE

Demco, Inc. 38-293

1. Folklore
2. Animals - Folklore

LANDSCAPES of LEGEND

FABULOUS BEASTS

—— ✦ The facts and the fables ✦ ——

Finn Bevan
Illustrated by Diana Mayo

CHILDREN'S PRESS®
A Division of Grolier Publishing
LONDON • NEW YORK • HONG KONG • SYDNEY
DANBURY, CONNECTICUT

Text © Finn Bevan 1997
Illustrations © Diana Mayo 1997

First American Edition by
Franklin Watts
A Division of Grolier Publishing Co., Inc.
Sherman Turnpike
Danbury, Connecticut 06813

Series editor: Rachel Cooke
Art director: Robert Walster
Designer: Mo Choy
Picture research: Sarah Moule

Library of Congress Cataloging-in-Publication Data
Bevan, Finn.
    Fabulous Beasts / Finn Bevan : illustrated by Diana Mayo.
        p.   cm. -- (Landscapes of legend)
    Includes index.
    Summary: A collection of traditional tales featuring animals, from
such places as West Africa, Brazil, and the Arctic.
    ISBN 0-516-20349-5
    1. Tales. 2. Animals--Folklore. [1. Folklore. 2. Animals-
-Folklore.] I. Mayo, Diana, ill. II. Title. III. Series.
PZ81..B47Fab 1997
[398.28'52]--dc21   96-45196
                                                                    CIP
                                                                     AC

Printed in Singapore

Picture acknowledgments:
Bruce Coleman pp. 14 (Staffan Widstrand), 18t (Hans Reinhard),
18b (Joe McDonald), 24t (Luiz Claudio Marigo)
Werner Forman Archive pp. 24c (National Museum of
Anthropology, Mexico), 26b (Alaska Gallery of Eskimo Art)
Hutchison Library p. 11 (Isabella Tree)
Image Bank p. 26t (Ocean Images/Giddings)
NHPA p. 10 (ANT/Kelvin Aitken)
ZEFA pp. 6t (Heilman), 15 (Damm)

Contents

✦

Spirits and Symbols

Animals, large and small, real and imaginary, play an important part in myths and legends from around the world. They are seen as powerful spirits, connecting people with their gods, or used as symbols of many human qualities. This reflects the vital role animals play in people's lives. For example, in places where people live close to nature, there is a special relationship between hunters and prey. It is no surprise that prehistoric hunters painted animals on cave walls and no doubt they told many animal stories. Their very lives depended on the fabulous beasts around them.

Fabulous Beasts

Many animals are used as symbols of particular qualities and powers that their behavior or appearance suggest. In ancient Greece, the owl was the symbol of Athena, goddess of wisdom. The owl's reputation for wisdom comes from its nocturnal (active at night) lifestyle. This was likened to the way studious scholars were known to study long into the night.

Similarly, because people admired lions for their great strength and power over other animals, these great cats have become symbols of leadership and the guardian animals of royalty.

Animals are often linked to a particular god, and many are worshiped as the messengers of the gods, or as gods or spirits in their own right. In ancient Egypt, cats were sacred to Bastet, goddess of love and motherhood, who was often shown as a cat. Killing a cat was a serious crime.

In some religions, people believe that, when you die, your soul may be reborn in another body, human or animal, depending on how you have lived your previous life. The Aztecs thought that the souls of dead warriors were reborn as hummingbirds. The San people of the Kalahari Desert believe hunters are reborn as antelopes.

Spider Tricksters

For its small size, the spider has amazing skill and cunning. It spins its delicate web, then lies in wait to trap a passing fly. Some spiders are nimble hunters, darting after insects on the ground. Others are more ingenious still, trapping their prey in silken nets. No wonder that the spider plays a leading role in many myths.

Spinning a Yarn

Spiders belong to a group of animals called arachnids. They get their name from an ancient Greek princess, Arachne, who challenged the goddess Athena to a weaving contest. By rights, Arachne won but Athena was so furious with her that Arachne tried to hang herself. Just in time, Athena saved her and turned her into a spider so that her spinning skills would not be lost.

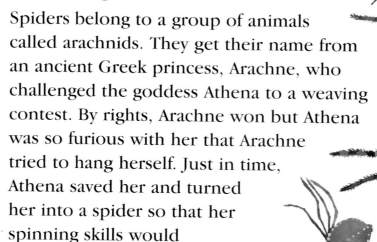

Anansi, the Spider

In African mythology, the spider uses its cunning to outwit animals much bigger than itself, even elephants and lions. The most famous spider of all is Anansi, the trickster hero of many tales.

How Anansi Became a Spider
African stories tell how Anansi was once a man who killed a ram that belonged to the king. The king found out about the crime and kicked Anansi so hard that he broke into a thousand pieces. These became a thousand spiders, which lurk in every nook and cranny.

Anansi and the Chameleon

This is the story of how Anansi the spider tricked the Chameleon and stole his field, and of how the Chameleon got his revenge.

◆

Anansi and the Chameleon lived in the same village. But Anansi had a large farm and many children, while the Chameleon had only one small field and lived alone. One year, however, the rain fell on the Chameleon's field and not at all on Anansi's farm. When Anansi asked to buy the Chameleon's field, the Chameleon said no. Anansi plotted his revenge.

When chameleons walk, they don't leave a trail, so there wasn't a path to the Chameleon's field. Anansi lost no time. Under cover of night, he trampled a wide path right from his house to the field. Then he claimed the field as his own, because the only path from it led straight to his door.

The Chameleon had been well and truly tricked. Now he had no field or food. Something had to be done. So he dug a huge, deep hole and covered it with a roof in which there was just one tiny hole. Then he made a magnificent cloak out of shiny flies, held together with vines. The village's chief himself liked the cloak so much he offered to buy it, but the Chameleon refused to sell.

"Don't worry," Anansi told the chief. "I'll get it for you. I've got plenty of money."

After some persuading, the Chameleon agreed to sell him the cloak, on one condition—that Anansi fill the seemingly tiny hole in his storehouse with food. So, all day long, Anansi's children poured grain into the hole but it never got any fuller. Day after day this went on, until all Anansi's grain was gone and he had to sell his sheep and cows to buy more grain.

At last, the Chameleon gave him the cloak. But such a long time had passed that the vines had rotted, and now all the shiny flies flew away. Anansi was left with just a few withered leaves, and no money or crops to his name. How the village laughed at him— he'd met his match for sure.

Shark Spirits of the Sea

Thousands of tiny tropical islands lie scattered across the South Pacific Ocean. The sea plays a crucial part in the islanders' lives. They rely on it for food and survival, and they fear and respect it for the awesome power of its waves and tides. Many of their gods are creatures of the sea, to be kept happy at all costs. Of all the animals featured in their stories one of the greatest is the shark.

Troublemakers

With its razor-sharp teeth and man-eating reputation, the great white shark is one of the most feared creatures in the sea. Some sea peoples worship sharks as powerful spirits. In Hawaii, stories are told of *mano-kanaka*, sharks who appear in human form to make trouble on land.

Other sea spirits take the form of sea snakes, crabs, turtles, whales, and hermit crabs.

Shark Magic

Pearl divers in Sri Lanka used to pay "shark-charmers" to protect themselves from attack. The shark-charmer was a magician who cast spells that sent the sharks to sleep while the divers worked.

Testing Times

In Papua New Guinea, boys have to catch a shark to prove their manhood. They set out alone in narrow canoes, armed only with a rope tied to a piece of wood. They "call" the shark by tapping the wood on the surface of the water. Then they lasso it with the rope, drag it into the canoe, and kill it. No one is sure why the sharks come. They seem to be hypnotized by the tapping.

Gentle Giants

The largest shark, and the biggest fish, is the enormous whale shark. It can grow over 49 ft (15 m) long and weigh 40 tons. Despite its huge size, the whale shark is a gentle giant. It lives solely on tiny plants and animals and is so harmless it even lets human divers ride on its back! The Fijian god of fishing, Dakuwaqa, takes the form of a basking shark, a close relation of the whale shark.

How the Great Shark God Met His Match

This is a story from Fiji, in the South Pacific.

◆

The deep blue sea around Fiji is ruled by sharks. And the great god of the sharks is called Dakuwaqa, a big, brave, but quarrelsome beast.

Each of the islands of Fiji once had a guardian, most often a shark. No one could approach the island, unless he said so. All the guardian sharks paid tribute to Dakuwaqa. He'd fought them all and beaten them, one by one. But Dakuwaqa had never fought the guardian of Long Island. This guardian, his friends told him, was even stronger and braver than he.

"We'll soon see about that!" roared Dakuwaqa, as he sped away. No one in the sea was mightier than he.

As he neared the island, a strange, low voice called him from the shore. It seemed to be coming from a tree. Dakuwaqa was frightened, for the first time in his life.

"So, at last, you've come," the voice whispered. "How I wish I could fight you myself. Instead, I must trust my faithful guardian. He'll soon teach you a lesson."

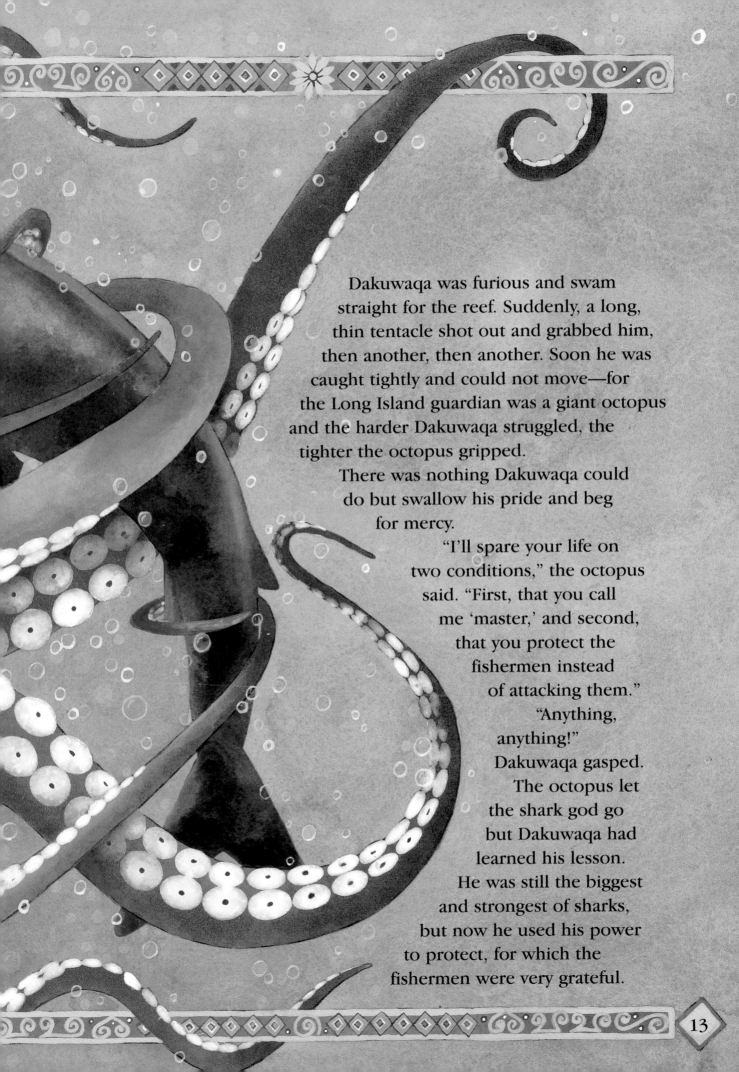

Dakuwaqa was furious and swam straight for the reef. Suddenly, a long, thin tentacle shot out and grabbed him, then another, then another. Soon he was caught tightly and could not move—for the Long Island guardian was a giant octopus and the harder Dakuwaqa struggled, the tighter the octopus gripped.

There was nothing Dakuwaqa could do but swallow his pride and beg for mercy.

"I'll spare your life on two conditions," the octopus said. "First, that you call me 'master,' and second, that you protect the fishermen instead of attacking them."

"Anything, anything!" Dakuwaqa gasped. The octopus let the shark god go but Dakuwaqa had learned his lesson. He was still the biggest and strongest of sharks, but now he used his power to protect, for which the fishermen were very grateful.

An Animal in Armor

Because of their tough, armor-plated shells and sturdy, pillar-like legs, tortoises are seen as symbols of strength in many myths. Often they appear in giant form, able to bear the whole world on their backs. In fact, their bony shells are used as protection against the crushing jaws of their enemies.

Tortoise Disguise

Hindus believe that the god Vishnu, the protector of the universe, has appeared on Earth ten times, in ten different disguises. Each time, he comes to save the world from disaster. In his second incarnation (appearance), Vishnu appeared as the tortoise Kurma and carried a mountain on his back.

The Weight of the World

In some Native American myths, the world is built out of mud on the back of a giant turtle, the only animal strong enough to carry its weight. In others, a huge tree linking the different parts of the universe is said to grow on the back of a giant turtle. Some Native American tales say that the rumble of earthquakes is caused by a giant turtle shaking its shell.

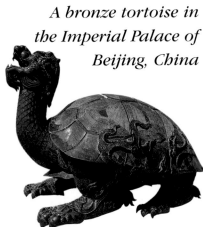

A bronze tortoise in the Imperial Palace of Beijing, China

One of Four

In Chinese mythology, the tortoise is one of the Four Sacred Creatures. The others are all imaginary beasts— the unicorn, dragon and phoenix. The tortoise symbolized long life (tortoises can live for more than 150 years) military might and was also an emblem of the Chinese royal family. It was believed that a race of giant tortoises once anchored the islands in the sea.

How a Tortoise Saved the World

This is a Chinese story about the tortoise's great strength.

◆

Long, long ago, when the world was new, the goddess Nu Gua came down from Heaven to live on Earth. There was no one else there, and Nu Gua soon grew lonely. So the goddess made herself some friends—the first people—and was never lonely again.

Time passed peacefully, then one day, a quarrel broke out between the fire god and ruler of the universe, Zhu Rong, and the water god, Gong Gong. The fire god ruled firmly but fairly, and Gong Gong, an ugly creature with a snake's body and a human head covered with bright red hair, hated him. He challenged him to a fight to see who was the most powerful. The contest was brief—Gong Gong was well and truly beaten.

In his anger and frustration, Gong Gong butted the Imperial Mountain with his head, and the mountain collapsed in a pile of rubble. Now, this was one of the mountains that held up the sky. When it fell down, a great jagged hole was torn in the sky, and great jagged cracks appeared in the ground. Fire and water poured out of them, drowning whole villages and burning crops.

Nu Gua could not stand idly by. She could not bear to see the people she'd made suffer so. She quickly went to a riverbed and picked up some pebbles and used them to plug the hole in the sky. But how could she stop it from collapsing again? There was only one animal strong enough to help. So Nu Gua found a giant tortoise and used it instead of the Imperial Mountain to prop up the heavens. And peace was restored to the world.

Flight of the Spirit Birds

For centuries the Native Americans of the northwest coast lived by hunting and fishing. From the sea came fish, seals, and sea birds. From the forests came caribou, eagles, and bears. Many myths grew up around these animals. Perhaps surprisingly, the scavenging raven is one of the most popular characters in these stories.

Animal Totem

Some Native American tribes believe that animal spirits are close to their own because their ancestors had been transformed from animals into humans. Each tribe has its own animal founder, often seen carved on totem poles. These totem animals—ravens, bears, eagles, blue jays, and mink— are worshiped as guardian spirits.

Souls in Flight

In many cultures, because they can fly, birds represent the flight of the human soul between this world and the next. In some Native American myths, the souls of the dead take the shape of owls.

The Mighty Thunderbird

Native Americans tell how thunderstorms are caused by a gigantic eagle called the Thunderbird. The rumble of thunder is the beating of the Thunderbird's wings. Lightning flashes from its eyes and beak. Despite its awesome power, the Thunderbird is a good spirit, bringing storms that stop the Earth from drying up.

The Clever Raven

The Raven appears in both human and bird form in Native American mythology. Many stories tell of Raven's greedy, thieving ways. But he is greatly admired for his intelligence and cunning, which he uses to outwit his enemies. Raven is also worshiped as the bringer of fire and light.

Raven Steals the Moon

*This Native American story tells of
Raven's thieving and cunning nature.*

◆

Once upon a time, there was
an old fisherman who lived
with his daughter on an island
far away to the north. His most
precious possession was a large
box in which he kept a very bright
light, called the Moon.

Now, the greedy Raven heard
about the wonderful light, and he
wanted it for himself. So he used
his magic to change into a leaf,
growing on a bush near the
fisherman's house. When the
fisherman's daughter came out
to pick berries from the bush, she
tugged the twig on which the leaf
grew, and it fell into her basket.
Later that day, and quite by chance,
she ate the leaf in her bowl of
berries. But that was not the end
of Raven's cunning plan.

Some time later, the fisherman's
daughter had a baby, with glossy,
dark skin and a strange, hooked
nose, like that of a bird.

As soon as the child was old enough to talk, he began to cry for the Moon. "Moon, oh shining Moon," he called, as he tapped on its box.

At first no one took any notice. But the crying continued, and the fisherman said to his daughter, "Give him the light to play with, if that's what he wants."

So the daughter opened the box. And inside there was another box, and another, until there were ten in all, each one most beautifully carved and painted. Inside the tenth box was a fine net with one final box nestled inside. The fisherman's daughter pulled it free and opened the lid. Suddenly the house was filled with shining white light, and inside the box they saw the Moon, gleaming and round, like a ball. She threw the ball toward her son, who caught and cradled it in his arms.

For a few days, the boy seemed happy. Then he began to cry again. He wanted to see the night sky and the stars, he said. But at night the sky was hidden by a board placed over the smoke hole in the roof.

"Open the smoke hole and let him look," his grandfather said.

So the fisherman's daughter opened the smoke hole. No sooner had she done so than the boy changed back into the Raven. And, with the Moon held firmly in his beak, off he flew into the night. Some way away from the fisherman's house, he landed on a mountaintop. Then he opened his beak and threw the Moon into the sky, where it remains, gleaming and white, to this very day.

Raven Creates the World

This story shows Raven using his skill and intelligence to create a new and better world.

◆

In the beginning, Raven made the world, everything in it, all the people, and totem poles too.

But first, a great flood drowned the Earth and destroyed the evil on it. One day, when the flood had gone down, Raven landed on a sandy shore. There he found a gigantic clamshell, full of tiny creatures, all quaking with fear and dread. They had survived the flood inside their shell, and they didn't want to leave its safety.

But Raven used smooth-sounding words and persuaded them out. They spread far and wide to explore the new and better world the flood had left behind. And eventually they changed and grew to become the world's first people. And Raven brought them salmon to eat and juicy ripe berries and other gifts, which, to this day, are greatly prized among them.

Lords of the Jungle

In the Central and South American rain forests, the jaguar rules supreme. Its strength, cunning, and skill at hunting are feared and worshiped by the local people. Not only is the jaguar the master of the animals, it is also a powerful spirit, representing life itself.

Jaguar Warriors

In Mayan and later Aztec times, the best and bravest warriors were known as jaguar knights and wore uniforms made of jaguar skins. Even today, hunters wear necklaces of jaguar teeth as symbols of strength.

A Mayan carving of a jaguar knight (the figure on the right) receiving a jaguar headdress from his wife.

The First Beings

Many rain forest people believe that the Sun made the world in the shape of a giant maloca (a traditional, communal house). The very first beings were the huge anaconda snakes. These turned into people named after forest animals, like tapir, armadillo, and jaguar. At first, people and animals lived together. Then the people discovered fire, and they went their separate ways.

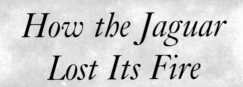

How the Jaguar Lost Its Fire

This jaguar story is from the rain forests of Brazil.

The very first people did not have fire. They ate their meat raw or warmed it in the Sun. One day, a boy climbed up a cliff to steal eggs from a macaw's nest. But someone pushed his ladder away, and he was left stranded.

Some days later, a jaguar passed by. It rescued the boy from the cliff and promised not to eat him. "You can be my new hunting companion," it said.

So the boy went home with the jaguar. And there he ate meat, roasted over a fire, and learned to make a bow and arrow. Then one day, when the jaguar was away, the boy killed the jaguar's wife with an arrow, stole some meat and an ember from the fire and ran back to his village. When the men of the village saw the boy's gifts, they went back to the jaguar's house. Not only did they steal the fire but all the bows and arrows too. So from that day, jaguars had to eat their meat raw and hunt with their teeth and claws, while people now ate their meat cooked and hunted with weapons.

Souls of the Ice

For the Inuit people who live around the icy Arctic Ocean, life is a constant struggle against the elements. Their survival depends on the frozen world around them, and they hold it in great respect. Particularly important are the animals—seals, walruses, fish, whales, and polar bears—on which they depend for food and materials. Many Inuit myths feature these animals.

Hunters and Prey

The Inuit believe that every animal and bird has a soul that must be respected. For this reason, hunters have a special relationship with their prey because one gives up its life for the other's benefit.

When an animal is killed, the hunters dance and sing to thank its spirit for its meat and skin in the hope that it will return to Earth to be hunted again. People also make carvings of animals in bone and ivory, to encourage them to visit their hunting grounds and to bring the hunters luck.

An Inuit carving of two polar bears fighting.

Polar Bear

The most powerful animal spirit is that of the polar bear, who is known as Nanok, the "great wanderer." It drifts for hundreds of miles on rafts of ice, in search of seals for food. Its spirit is believed to be closest to that of humans. When a polar bear is killed, the hunters dance in its skin and offer its spirit food to lessen its anger.

Goddess of the Sea

In Inuit mythology, the most important goddess is Sedna, the spirit of the sea. From her home in the ocean depths, she sends out the animals to be hunted. Every Inuit group has a magician, called an *angakok*. If the hunting is bad, he goes into a trance and sends his soul to visit Sedna to beg her to release more animals.

How the Seals Came to Be

This is an Inuit story about how the goddess Sedna created the animals in the sea.

◆

There was once a pretty young girl called Sedna who lived with her father by the sea. Many young men asked to marry her, but she refused them all. Then, one day, a handsome hunter paddled by in his canoe. He called to Sedna from the sea:

"Come with me to the land of the birds where no one ever goes hungry or cold, and I'll surround you with precious things."

Sedna still wasn't sure, but the precious things sounded very tempting. She got into the stranger's boat and off they sped.

The stranger was no ordinary man but a bird spirit in disguise. When Sedna found out his true identity, she wept with despair and begged to go home. But the bird spirit would not let her leave.

Now Sedna's father set out in his boat to find his daughter. Sedna was alone and overjoyed to see him. Together, they set off for home.

When the bird spirit returned and found Sedna gone, he was furious. His anger grew when the wind told him what had happened. He changed into a bird and soon caught up with the little boat.

"Let me see Sedna, I beg you," he croaked.

But her father refused, and the bird spread his wings and soared away into the darkness. Suddenly a terrible storm swept across the sea. Sedna's father was terrified and fear of the bird spirit gripped his heart. This was surely his revenge. There was only one thing to do—he picked up his daughter and threw her overboard, to calm the angry sea.

Sedna held on to the side of the boat, as tightly as she could. But her father grabbed his ax and cut off all her fingers. While Sedna sank beneath the waves, where she has lived ever since, her fingers turned into the seals, and the whales, and the walruses. And this is how the creatures of the sea came to be.

Notes and Explanations

Who's Who

ANCIENT GREEKS: The people who lived in Greece from about 2,000 BC. Theirs was a highly advanced civilization, famous for its arts, science, and trade. Myths formed an important part of ancient Greek religion, explaining the nature of their gods. We know these myths through the works of ancient Greek writers, such as the poet Homer, who lived in about the 8th century BC.

ANCIENT EGYPTIANS: The people who lived in Egypt, along the banks of the River Nile, from about 5,000 to 30 BC. Famous for their temples, pyramids, and tombs, these have provided a huge amount of information about the myths, beliefs, and lifestyle of ancient Egypt. The ancient Egyptians worshipped many gods and goddesses, who controlled all aspects of nature and daily life.

AZTECS: The people who lived in Mexico from the 13th to 16th century until their civilization was destroyed by Spanish invaders. Their gods included the Sun to whom they sacrificed human hearts and blood.

HINDUS: Followers of the Hindu religion, which began in India some 4,500 years ago. About 80 per cent of Indians are Hindus. They believe in a wide variety of gods and in reincarnation (being born again after you die). The aim of a Hindu's life is to break free of the cycle of birth and rebirth, so gaining salvation.

INUIT: The name given to the native people who live around the Arctic Ocean. In their own language, "Inuit" means "the People."

MAYA: The people, famous for their advanced civilization, who lived in Central America from about 500 BC to the 15th century AD.

NATIVE AMERICANS: The original inhabitants of North America who migrated from Asia about 50,000 years ago. Today they make up less than 1 per cent of the U.S. population. Since European settlers arrived in the 15th century, they have struggled to keep their lands and preserve their traditional lifestyle.

POLYNESIANS: The original inhabitants of the islands of the eastern and central South Pacific Ocean. These include Hawaii, Tonga, Samoa, and New Zealand.

SAN PEOPLE: A nomadic people who live in the Kalahari Desert in southern Africa.

What's What

Strictly speaking, fables, legends, and myths are all slightly different. But the three terms are often used to mean the same thing—a symbolic story or a story with a message.

FABLE: A short story, not based in fact, that often has animals as its central characters, and a strong moral lesson to teach.

LEGEND: An ancient, traditional story based on supposed historical figures or events.

MYTH: A story not based in historical fact but one that uses supernatural characters to explain natural phenomena, such as the weather, night and day, the rising tides, and so on. Before the scientific facts were known, ancient people used myths to make sense of the world around them.

GUARDIAN: Someone or something who watches over and protects a person or place. Guardians can be people, animals or spirits.

SOUL: The inner part or spirit of a person or animal, as opposed to its physical body. Many people believe the soul gives life to the body and, unlike the body, it never dies.

SYMBOL: Something which stands for or represents another thing. For example, owls are a symbol of wisdom. Symbols often makes things easier to picture or understand.

Where's Where

The map below shows where in the world the places named in this book are found.

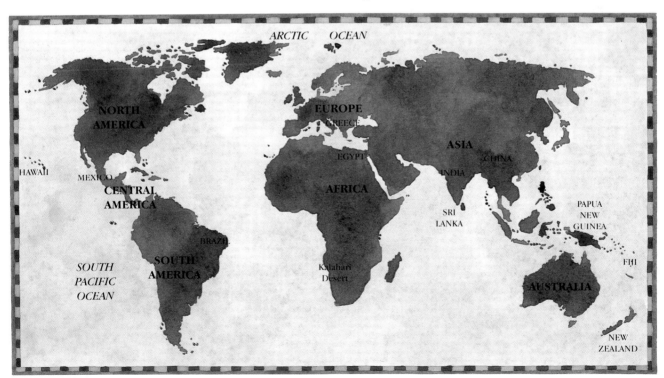

Index